This book belongs to:

_____

To my dreamy daughters Violet, Primose, and Wisteria

This book is based on the TV episode "Humbug," written by Scott Kraft,
from the animated TV series *Miss Spider's Sunny Patch Friends* on Nick Jr.,
a Nelvana Limited/Absolute Pictures Limited co-production in association
with Callaway Arts & Entertainment, based on the Miss Spider books by David Kirk.

Nicholas Callaway, President and Publisher
Cathy Ferrara, Managing Editor and Production Director
Toshiya Masuda, Art Director • Nelson Gómez, Director of Digital Technology
Joya Rajadhyaksha, Editor • Amy Cloud, Editor
Raphael Shea, Senior Designer • Krupa Jhaveri, Designer
Bill Burg, Digital Artist • Christina Pagano, Digital Artist • Dominique Genereux, Digital Artist
Keith McMenamy, Digital Artist

Special thanks to the Nelvana staff, including Doug Murphy, Scott Dyer, Tracy Ewing, Pam Lehn,
Tonya Lindo, Mark Picard, Jane Sobol, Luis Lopez, Eric Pentz, and Georgina Robinson.

Library of Congress Cataloging-in-Publication Data available upon request.

Distributed in the United States by Penguin Young Readers Group.

Visit Callaway Arts & Entertainment at www.callaway.com.

ISBN 978-0-448-45022-3

10 9 8 7 6 5 4 3 2 1   08 09 10 11

First edition, September 2006

Printed in China

Miss Spider's

HUMBUG!

David Kirk

CALLAWAY

NEW YORK

2008

Beneath the veil of shining stars,
Where insect angels dwell,

The dream bug glides with moonlit wings
Upon a cloudy swell.

Each solstice eve, she brings the joy
That dreamers long to know,

And sows her seeds of goodness
Where they're likeliest to grow.

With just a curl of frosty breath—
A whisper barely heard,

She fills your head with lovely dreams,
Then sails without a word

To lace her graceful, golden thread
In patterns through the night

Over, under, weaving wonder,
Winging out of sight.

The little bugs of Sunny Patch
Were studying the sky.

"We've all done our good deeds," said Squirt.
"She wouldn't pass us by!"

"I've been a nice bug," Bounce exclaimed,
"Polite and kind and stuff—

As good as I could be. Oh no! . . .
But was I good enough?"

Poor Bounce ran to his mother
And explained his dismal plight.

"I need to do a deed that's good,
And do it by tonight!"

Miss Spider smiled, "Dear Eunice
Sprained a pincer yesterday.

Why don't you gather winter food
And take it up her way?"

So out among the snowy fields
Bounce trudged behind his cart.

A heap of berries towered high
As gladness filled his heart.

Spiderus, creeping from his lair,
Beheld the tender treat.

"How fortunate!" he bellowed.
"You're in time for me to eat!"

"Don't eat me now, Spiderus, please!
I'm doing my good deed.

Collecting yummy berry snacks—
The earwigs are in need!

The dream bug's coming,"
   Bounce explained.
"I need to run, you see.

If I don't get my good deed done,
There'll be no dreams for me."

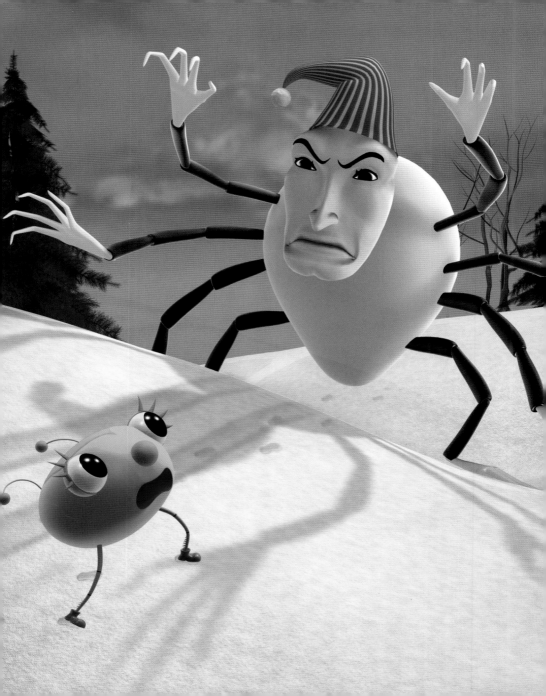

"The dream bug, bah!" Spiderus growled.
But then he changed his mind.

He cooed, "Dear boy, I'd like to help,
If you would be so kind.

You've done your deed, now don't
I need a dream bug visit, too?

Just drop this heavy burden.
I'll deliver it for you."

That night, in dreams, Bounce
   leapt through fruit,
Delicious, firm, and round,

While Shimmer soared among the starry
Clouds without a sound.

Wiggle dreamt he'd won a race.
Holley saw an angel's face.

Everybuggy's dream revealed
A glimpse of perfect grace.

Spiderus, dozing by his fire,
Content, was dreaming, too,

Of nasty tricks that he had played
And those he'd yet to do.

Like stealing food from little tykes—
What joy to hear them whine.

He stuffed their berries in his mouth
And laughed, "They're mine, all MINE!"

Devouring fruit from every branch,
He stuffed his bulging sack.

But as he gorged, the angry trees
Were grouping to attack.

They hurled their fruit like cannonballs.
The snow was stained with red.

He tumbled down the hillside
And woke screaming in his bed.

"Be still, my love, it's just a dream,"
Spindella whispered low.

"Then there's still time?" Spiderus gasped.
"Stand back, I have to go!"

He loaded berries on his sleigh,
And balanced even more,

Then piled them with a friendly note
By Eunice Earwig's door.

The deed was done. His spirits soared.
Returning to his lair,

It wasn't long before sweet dreams
Were swirling through the air.

He drifted off to Slumberland.
In just a little while

His grumpy sneer had disappeared—
Lips curled into a smile.

The grateful earwigs gathered 'round
To thank their gracious friend—

A hero warm and generous,
With eight strong hands to lend.

His hard, old heart was filled with pride.
His eyes welled up with tears.

A hundred insects sang his praise.
The village rang with cheers.